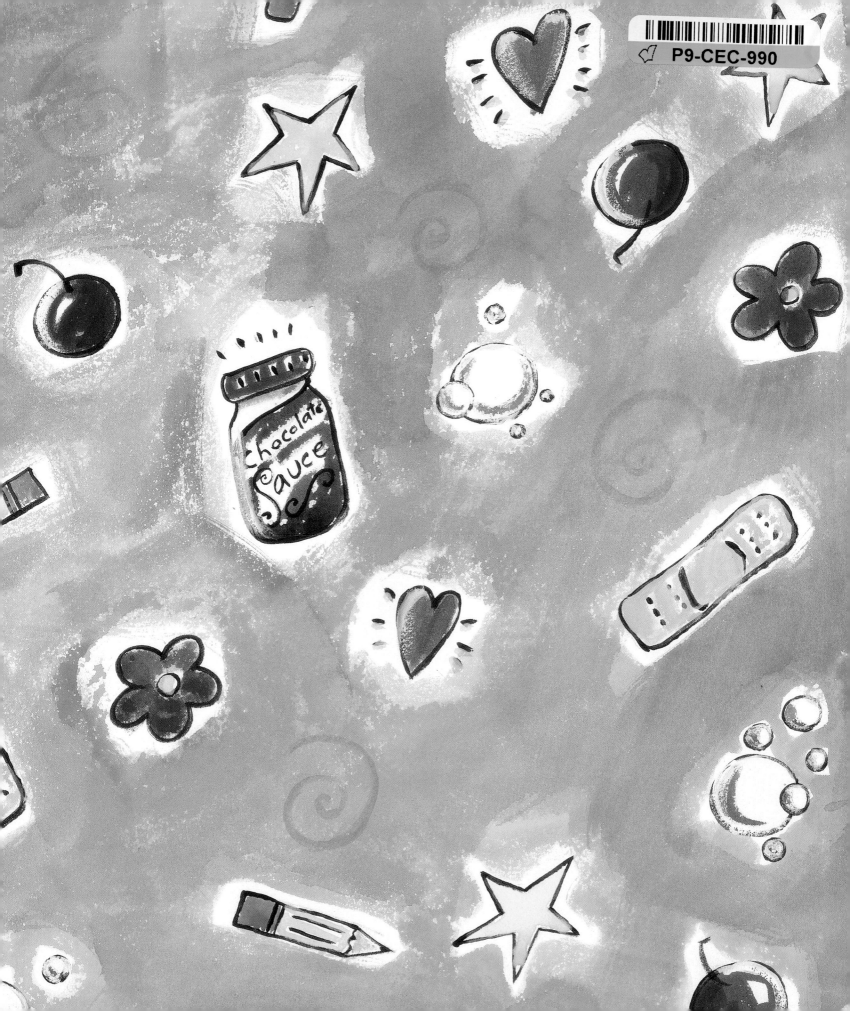

For my twins, Lindsay and Isabella.
Each of you is special, although you look alike.
—*Mom*

Dedicated with love to my sweet husband, Brian, and our angel dog,
Sally, for all their love and support.
—*Amanda*

Ahrens, Robin Isabel.
Dee and Bee / written by Robin Isabel Ahrens; illustrated by Amanda Haley.
First Edition
p.   cm.
Summary: Identical twins Dee and Bee enjoy fooling people by switching places with each other,
at school, in the neighborhood, and at bedtime.
ISBN 1-890817-26-0
[1. Twins Fiction. 2. Sisters Fiction. 3. Identity Fiction. 4. Stories in rhyme.]
I. Title II. Haley, Amanda, ill.
PZ8.3.A1235Dg   2000
[E]—dc21
99-37945   CIP

Creative Director: Bretton Clark
Designer: Rose Walsh
Editor: Margery Cuyler

Printed in Belgium

This book has a trade reinforced binding.

For games, links and more, visit our interactive Web site:
www.winslowpress.com

Dee and Bee

written by Robin Isabel Ahrens

illustrated by Amanda Haley

WINSLOW PRESS

Delray Beach, Florida • New York

Hello out there. My name is **Bee**.

I am a twin as you can see.

Here's my sister. She is Dee.

And Dee looks just the same as me.

Most people can't tell who is who,

unless we offer them a clue.

But lots of times we think it's fun

to say we are the other one.

When I ask to leave the class,
my teacher says, "Why do you ask?"

"You just came back inside, I think,
Or was it Dee who got a drink?"

WHO LEFT THE CLASSROOM, DEE OR BEE?

When I polish off my peas,
I want to eat some ice cream, PLEEESE!

My sitter says, "It can't be right that you have such an appetite."

WHO ATE THE ICE CREAM, DEE OR BEE?

Each year we visit Dr. Knott,
who tries to give me one more shot.

"Again?" I shout with great alarm.
"See the red mark on my arm?"

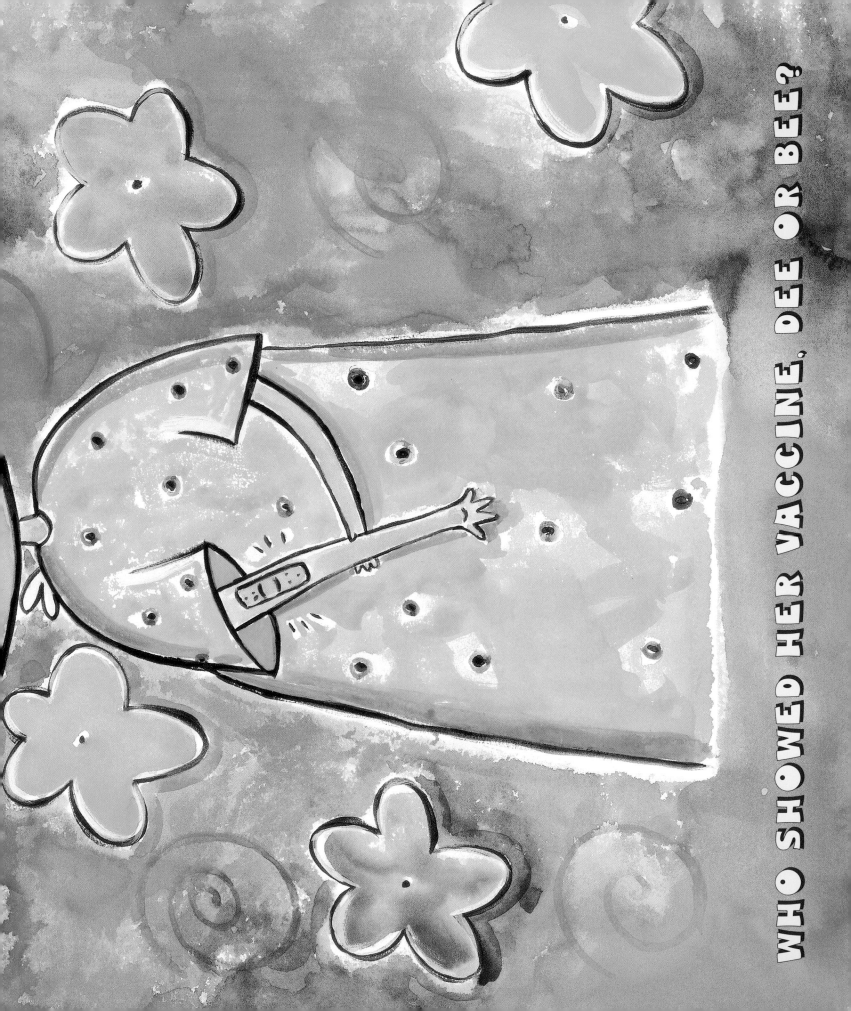

WHO SHOWED HER VACCINE, DEE OR BEE?

The trick of switching one another,
we also try on our big brother.

As I run by, he starts to shout,
"Didn't I just tag you out?"

WHO RAN THE BASES, DEE OR BEE?

At night when Mommy runs our bath,
we can't resist another laugh.

She grabs the soap, "Let's clean your face!"
But I fool Mom and switch my place.

WHO CHANGED PLACES, DEE OR BEE?

At last it's time to go to bed.
I wish I were a sleepyhead.
I'll count the sheep from one to three,

and hope they'll jump from Dee to me.

Yes, they can, with help from me.

Good night, sleep tight, my sister Dee!

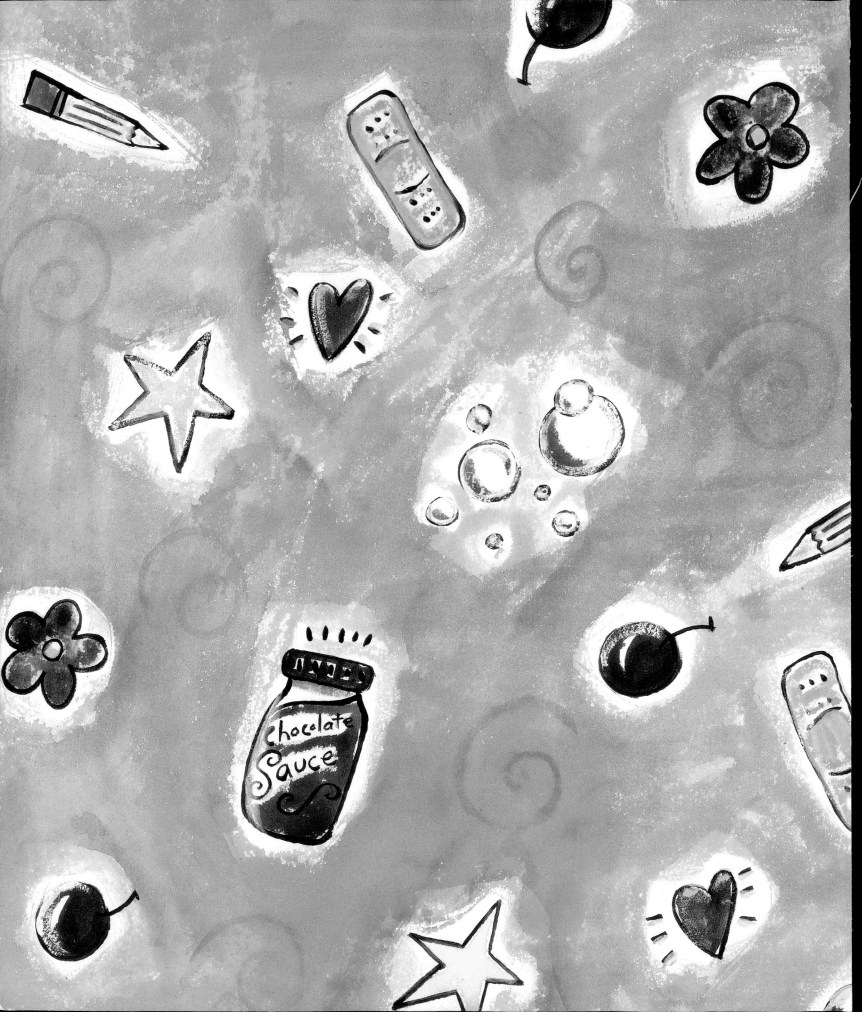